This Mardles Story Belongs To

.............Malachi.............

Don't Be Afraid Little Snail
By Ross Andrew Brown and Sophie Barnes
Illustrations by Reza
Digital magic by Harmony
Edited by Rachael Salt

Third Edition 2019
Second Edition 2018
First published and printed in 2017 by AliveLab LTD

ISBN: 978-0-9957053-1-9
Printed and bound in China: 003
Mardles.com

How to use this book

1) Download the free  app.

2) Point the device at any of the magic pages. Look out for the ✨ symbol.

3) The story magically comes to life in 4D.

4) Take control with the on screen arrows!

Download the free Mardles App from the app stores!
For compatible devices visit Mardles.com

At the end of the garden behind the shed,
Lives a snail named Sam with a little green head.

Sam is afraid of the big world outside,
So he stays in his shell where he's happy to hide.

Now and again he comes out for a peep,
When everything's quiet, and his friends are asleep.

Sam stays inside and sleeps through the day,
While lots of his friends go outside to play.

Inside his shell he's happiest there,
It's safe and it's warm and makes him less scared.

In his dreams he'd go out and have some fun too,
But that is something he's too scared to do!

He dreams of flying a plane in the sky,
Up through the clouds – flying so high.

He dreams of rowing a boat on the sea,
Or building a house up in a tree.

He dreams of adventure, he wants to get out,
But it seems there is so much to worry about.

One day Sam was sleeping when he heard a 'tap tap'
He woke with a start 'Whatever was that?'

He popped out his head and to his surprise,
Staring at him was a huge pair of eyes!

'P P Please go away' Sam said to the mouse,
'I really don't want to come out of my house.'

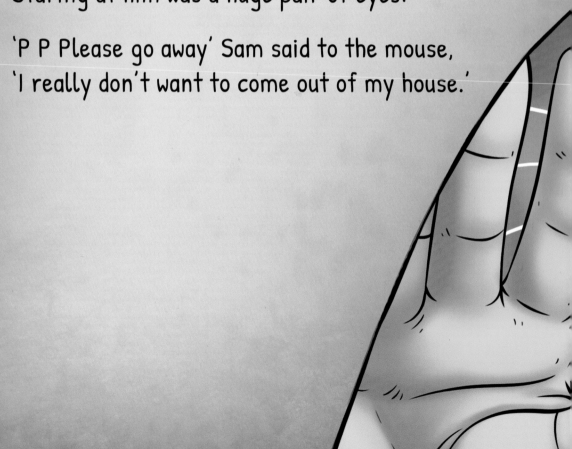

'Don't be afraid!' said the mouse with a stare,
'Your shell looks so pretty! Are you living in there?'

Sam shook and shivered as he replied,
'Why thank you kind mouse yes, I do live inside.'

The mouse then told Sam of adventures she'd had,
Sam started to think 'That doesn't sound bad!'

Out of his shell, slowly he crawled,
'Hooray! Well done you!' everyone called.

Sam was amazed, there was so much to see
He could finally be happy, adventurous and free

He had lots of questions about lots of things,
Like 'What are those creatures with beautiful wings?'

'They're pretty butterflies' his new friend replied
'They live near the flowers and fly in the sky.

We share the world with things great and small,
And it's everyone's job to look after it all.'

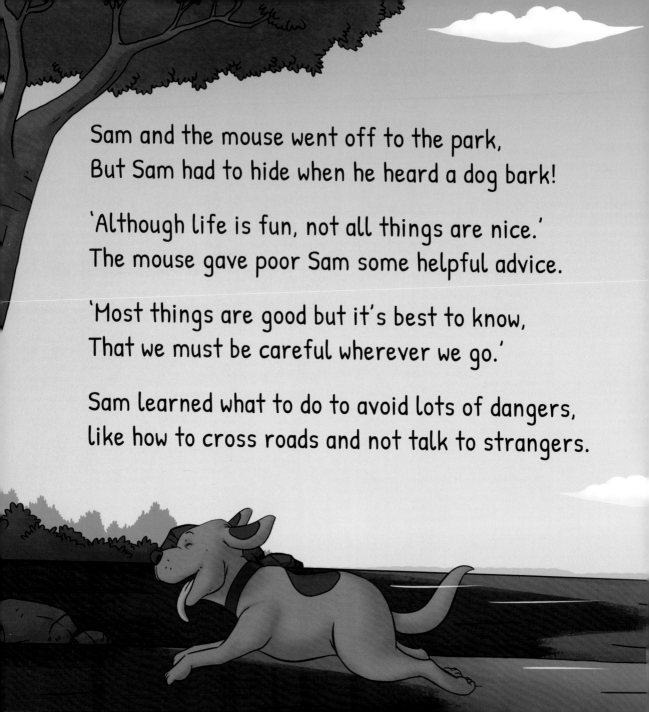

Sam and the mouse went off to the park,
But Sam had to hide when he heard a dog bark!

'Although life is fun, not all things are nice.'
The mouse gave poor Sam some helpful advice.

'Most things are good but it's best to know,
That we must be careful wherever we go.'

Sam learned what to do to avoid lots of dangers,
like how to cross roads and not talk to strangers.

After the park Sam was feeling quite brave,
He saw a nice cat and gave him a wave.

The cat waved right back! He wanted to meet,
(And looked both ways before crossing the street).

'I'm going shopping' the cat told the friends,
'I like to keep up with fashion and trends.

I think you'd look smart in a lovely top hat.'
So off went the snail, the mouse and the cat.

With his hat on his head it was time to return,
Back to the garden to share what he'd learned.

'Thank you, kind mouse! You've helped me to see,
Just how exciting the outside can be.'

'That's great' said the mouse 'it's not really scary,
Enjoy life out there but just do it carefully.'

'Now I'm Sam the brave, not at all like before!'
The scared little snail wasn't scared any more.

We hope that you have enjoyed bringing this story to life.

Share your experience with us!

Search for 'Mardles'

@MardlesLife

@MardlesLife

See what else we bring to life at
WWW.MARDLES.COM

Discover the whole range...

The Copycat Parrot

The Cow That Says 'How?'

Don't Be Afraid Little Snail

The Egg Who Couldn't Wait

Stanley The Seahorse